LOST AT THE WHITE HOUSE

A 1909 Easter Story

by Lisa Griest
illustrations by Andrea Shine

Carolrhoda Books / Minneapolis, Minnesota

To my grandma Rena for this story
To Gary for everything—L.G.

To my sister Vivian,
with whom I shared so many adventures—A.S.

This book is available in two editions:
Library binding by Carolrhoda Books, Inc.
Soft cover by First Avenue Editions
Carolrhoda Books, Inc., and First Avenue Editions
c/o The Lerner Group
241 First Avenue North
Minneapolis, Minnesota 55401

Library of Congress Cataloging-in-Publication Data

Griest, Lisa.
    Lost at the White House: a 1909 Easter story / by
Lisa Griest; illustrations by Andrea Shine.
        p. cm. — (Carolrhoda on my own book)
    Summary: When Rena gets lost at the 1909 White House
Easter egg roll, a guard takes her to meet President
William Taft.
    ISBN 0-87614-726-0 (lib. bdg.)
    ISBN 0-87614-632-9 (pbk.)
    [1. Presidents—Fiction. 2. Taft, William H.
(William Howard), 1857–1930—Fiction. 3. Easter eggs—
Fiction.] I. Shine, Andrea, ill. II. Title. III. Series.
PZ7.G86244Lo 1994
[E]—dc20   93-7945
                                              CIP
                                               AC

Manufactured in the United States of America
1 2 3 4 5 6 – I/SP – 99 98 97 96 95 94

Author's Note

This story is based on my grandmother Rena's experience at the 1909 White House Easter egg roll. The first Easter egg roll at the White House took place in 1879, and by 1909, close to ten thousand children attended the annual event. The tradition has continued through the years.

For children, the chance to frolic on the rolling south lawn of the White House on Easter Monday has made the egg roll one of the most popular events of the year. Admission is free, but guards bar entrance to any adult not accompanied by a child. The *Washington Post* noted in 1909 that more than one resourceful boy was seen charging unaccompanied adults up to a quarter to "take them inside." The clever youngsters would then race back out and "work the same trick at the gate on the other side."

For the gardeners and groundskeepers charged with cleaning up the thousands of broken eggshells, empty lunch boxes, newspapers, and popped balloons, the Easter egg roll has not always been so popular. "It's a nasty mess," the head gardener of the White House said in 1909, "and it means a lot of work cleaning up and putting things ship-shape, but I'm blest if watchin' it wasn't worth all the trouble."

"You listen to me, Rena," said Rose.

"Don't get dirty.

Don't get lost.

And don't bother me today."

Rena and Rose were going
to the White House.
It was the day of
the Easter egg roll.
Rena knew Rose was mad.
Rose was fourteen.
She did not want to bring her
nine-year-old sister along.
But it was Rena's first
Easter egg roll.
Nothing was going
to spoil it for her.

Clang! Clang! went the streetcars.
They were filled with children
carrying baskets of Easter eggs.
Honk! Honk! went the motorcars.
Each car carried children dressed in
bright Easter colors.

Next came the carriages,
pulled by horses.
They were chased by boys
trying to catch a ride.

At the White House gates,

men in tall hats stood on guard.

"Balloons for sale!"

sang the toy vendors.

"Hokey-pokeys!"

sang the ice cream vendors.

"Look, Rose! Ice cream!" shouted Rena.

"No!" scolded Rose.

"Now hurry up or I'll take you home!"

Rena and Rose walked

to the end of the long line.

Rena could hear the friendly voices
of the guards.
"Smiles and colored eggs only!"
they shouted.
"You must be a child or be
with a child to come in today."

A man without a child
tried to squeeze by.
The guards were not friendly anymore.
"Didn't you hear me, sir?"
one of them said.
"I just want to see what it looks
like," the man said.
"Step aside, sir," said the guard.
He seemed to grow much bigger
as he said this.
The man looked angry.
But he turned and walked away.

Finally Rena and Rose reached the
front of the line.
The guards just smiled at them as
they stepped through the gates.

In the distance, Rena could see the
White House.
She had never been this close to the
president's house before.

The lawn in front of the White House
was covered with children.
There were children chasing eggs and
children chasing other children.
Eggs were tumbling down hills, with
children tumbling after them.
High above, in the trees, squirrels
chattered noisily over the ruckus.

Rena carried her basket
to the top of a hill.
She picked out a pink egg.
She set the egg on the ground and
gave it a push.

The egg rolled and bounced all the
way to the bottom of the hill.
Rena ran down the hill
to get her egg.

A group of boys was ting nearby.

"Look, there's the president!"

one boy said.

"That's not the president,"

said another boy.

"He's not big enough.

Presidents are all as big as giants."

"Yes," said a third boy.

"And the president never goes

anywhere without guards with guns."

Guards with guns!

Rena thought about

the guard at the gates.

Did he have a gun? she wondered.

He sure looked angry

when the man tried— THUD!

A boy rolling down the hill
knocked Rena off her feet.
"Oh, look what you've done!"
Rena cried.

All of the things had spilled
out of her basket.
Her white dress was stained green
at the knees.
Rose had told her not to get dirty.
Rose was not going to be happy.
Rose!
Where was Rose?

Rena did not see her sister anywhere.
There were hundreds of
white Easter dresses.
There were hundreds of pink and
yellow and blue Easter bonnets.
There were hundreds of parasols.
The parasols protected faces
from the sun.
And they blocked faces
from Rena's eyes.

Rena searched frantically
for her sister.
Was that her?

The girl had on the same
white-and-blue dress that Rose wore.
She had the same color hair.
Rena ran to the girl.
"Thank goodness I found you!"
she cried.

The girl looked at Rena
with surprise.
She was not Rose.

Rena sat down under an elm tree
to catch her breath.
Now she was really in trouble.
She was dirty.
And she was lost.
Rena sighed and stood up.
At least she wasn't bothering Rose.
She straightened her dress.
Then she set off to look for Rose
more carefully.

Soon Rena noticed she was not very
far from the White House.
She stopped and looked up at the
big white building.
What was it like inside?
she wondered.

Would ai_____ _____ __ __ _

just one peek

Rena started acro_ _he lawn toward

the White House.

She looked behind her to make sure

no one was watching.

Then she turned and walked

right into a guard.

It was one of the guards
from the front gates.
This time he was not smiling.
"Where do you think you're going?"
Rena looked up at the
man's stern face.
"I'm lost," she said.
"You had better come with me,"
said the guard.
He took her by the arm.
Rena was too worried to notice
where the guard was taking her.
What happened to people who were
caught sneaking around
the White House?

Rena's feet climbed
a flight of twisting stairs.
She looked around.
She must be inside the White House!

They entered a beautiful room.
It was shaped just like
an Easter egg.

The guard told Rena to wait.

Then he left the room.

Rena looked out the window.

She could see the

children on the lawn.

How she wished she were with them.

All of a sudden, huge man
burst into the room.
He had a thick white mustache.
It curved down like a walrus's
over his top lip.
At least two chins stuck out
over his collar.

"What is your name?" the man boomed.

"Re-Rena," Rena said
in a small voice.

"Who did you come with?" he asked.

"My sister, Rose," said Rena.
The man frowned.

"And where is this sister of yours?"

"She's outside," answered Rena.

"They told me you were sneaking
around outside.
I thought you might like to talk to
me," said the man.

Rena was too scared to speak.

She did not want to talk to this

huge, frightening man.

She wanted to go home.

She wanted to be bothering Rose.

She wanted to be anywhere but here.

"Do you know who this is?"

asked the guard.

Rena shook her head.

"My name is William Taft,"

said the large man.

Rena looked up in surprise.

"Why, you are the president of the

United States!" she said.

The president laughed.

"That's right," he said, "I am."

Rena looked at the man.

He *was* a giant.

This must be the president.

Rena told the president that this was
her first Easter egg roll.
And she told him how
she had gotten lost.
While Rena talked to the president,
the guard went to find Rose.
Then it was time to say good-bye.

The guard came back
to take Rena to the gates.
She would meet Rose there.
The president shook Rena's hand.
"Good-bye, Rena," he said.
"It was very good to meet you."
"I'm glad I got to meet you, too,"
Rena said.

Rose was waiting at the gates.

"Oh, Rose, you won't believe what happened," said Rena.

"I met—"

"Be quiet!" scolded Rose.

"Do you know how worried I've been?
I knew you were too young
to come today.

My whole Easter has been ruined!"

"But Rose," said Rena, "I met—"

"I don't want to hear another word
from you," said Rose.

"You will never get to go to the
Easter egg roll again.

Not if I can help it."

Rena just smiled.

She was not worried.

She knew that no other Easter egg
roll could ever match this one.